Mystery Mob
and the Monster
on the Moor

Roger Hurn

Illustrated by
Stik

RISING STARS

Essex County Council Libraries

Rising Stars UK Ltd.
22 Grafton Street, London W1S 4EX
www.risingstars-uk.com

The right of Roger Hurn to be identified as the author of this work
has been asserted by him in accordance with the Copyright, Design
and Patents Act 1988.

Published 2007

Cover design: Button plc
Illustrator: Stik, Bill Greenhead for Illustration
Text design and typesetting: Andy Wilson
Publisher: Gill Budgell
Publishing manager: Sasha Morton
Editor: Catherine Baker
Series consultant: Cliff Moon

British Library Cataloguing in Publication Data.
A CIP record for this book is available from the British Library

ISBN: 978-1-84680-223-2

Printed in the UK by CPI Bookmarque, Croydon, CR0 4TD

FSC **Mixed Sources**
Product group from well-managed
forests and other controlled sources
www.fsc.org Cert no. TT-COC-002227
© 1996 Forest Stewardship Council

Contents

Meet the Mystery Mob

Name:

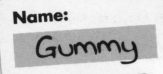
Gummy

FYI: Gummy hasn't got much brain – and even fewer teeth.

Loves: Soup.

Hates: Toffee chews.

Fact: The brightest thing about him is his shirt.

Name:

Lee

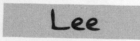

FYI: If Lee was any cooler he'd be a cucumber.

Loves: Hip-hop.

Hates: Hop-scotch.

Fact: He has his own designer label (which he peeled off a tin).

Name:

Rob

FYI: Rob lives in his own world – he's just visiting planet Earth.

Loves: Daydreaming.

Hates: Nightmares.

Fact: Rob always does his homework – he just forgets to write it down.

Name:

Dwayne

FYI: Dwayne is smarter than a tree full of owls.

Loves: Anything complicated.

Hates: Join-the-dots books.

Fact: If he was any brighter you could use him as a floodlight at football matches.

Name:

Chet

FYI: Chet is as brave as a lion with steel jaws.

Loves: Having adventures.

Hates: Knitting.

Fact: He's as tough as the chicken his granny cooks for his tea.

Name:

Adi

FYI: Adi is as happy as a football fan with tickets to the big match.

Loves: Telling jokes.

Hates: Moaning minnies.

Fact: He knows more jokes than a jumbo joke book.

Welcome to
Muckle Moor ...

Muckle Moor is a lonely place.
It's miles from anywhere,
and wherever you go,
it feels as though someone
is watching you.
Spooky!

But the Mystery Mob are going
to Muckle Moor. It's where Lee's
rich uncle lives, in a big, posh house.
The boys knock at the front door.

Adi   Wow! Just look at this place!
It's awesome!

Lee   Yeah – my uncle's got
a games room and
a wicked swimming pool, too.

Adi   Cool! Hey, what do you get
if a whole load of crooks
jump into a swimming pool?

Gummy   I don't know.

Adi   A crime wave!

Gummy   Doh!

Dwayne Shut up, you two –
here comes Lee's uncle.

But it isn't Lee's uncle who opens the door
– it's the butler.

Butler   Come in. The master of the house
is away, but he has left orders
for me to give you tea.
Follow me.

The butler takes the Mystery Mob
to the kitchen for their tea.
While they are tucking into
huge slices of chocolate cake
he gives them a warning.

Butler   Don't go out on the Moor alone –
or you might meet the monster
that lives there!

Chet   A monster? You're kidding us!

Butler   Not at all, young man.
The Monster of Muckle Moor
is real. But no one who has seen
the monster has ever lived
to tell the tale.

Dwayne   So how do you know
about it then?

The butler smiles but says nothing.
He glides out of the kitchen.

Lee   I think there's something funny
about that butler.

Gummy   Really? He doesn't make
me laugh.

The boys talk about what kind of monster could live on the moor.

Adi   If it's a dinosaur monster, it'll be a terror-dactyl!

Dwayne   Don't be daft. There are no such things as monsters.

Rob   You wouldn't say that if you'd met my teacher.

Chet   I'm not scared of monsters. We should go on a monster hunt!

Lee   It's getting dark. I'm not going out looking for monsters now. It's time we all went to bed.

Rob   Okay. But what do we do if we find a monster under our beds?

Gummy   Tell it not to snore!

Monster Hunt

Early next morning, Chet and Adi
wake up. The rest of the Mystery Mob
are still fast asleep. Chet wants
to go on a monster hunt.

Chet and Adi creep outside.
They see a couple of bicycles
by the garden wall.
There is a long piece of rope
on the ground.

Adi   It'll be much easier to search
for the monster if we borrow
these bikes. And we can
use this rope to tie
the monster up.

Chet   Great idea. Come on.
I'll race you to the Moor.
We can catch the monster
and be back for breakfast.

Adi   I bet the monster has rice creepies
and terri-fried eggs for breakfast.

The two boys
jump on the bikes and pedal off.
The sky is blue and the sun is shining.
But for some reason, Adi has the shivers.

Adi   I don't like it here.

Chet   Why – what's wrong with it?

Adi   Dunno – I just don't like
the spooky shadows from
those tall rocks. Listen –
what was that?

Chet   Just an old, dead tree rustling
in the wind. Don't be chicken, Adi!

Adi   We need a joke to cheer us up.
Hey, Chet, what's the best day
of the week to meet monsters?

Chet   No idea.

Adi   Frightday.

Chet   Doh! You're really scared,
            aren't you, Adi?

Adi   No! I just don't fancy being
            a Monster's Munch.

Chet   The monster won't eat you, Adi.
            You'd give him a belly ache.

For some reason this doesn't make Adi
feel any safer.

Run For Your Life!

Chet and Adi cycle along a dusty track.
The birds are singing. The air smells fresh
and sweet. Adi begins to relax.

Before long they come to an old cottage.

The cottage looks dark and gloomy.
Paint is peeling from the walls
and the windows are cracked.
There are holes in the roof
and weeds in the garden.
No birds are singing in the trees.

Adi   All this monster hunting is
          making me thirsty. Let's stop
          at this cottage and ask
          for a drink.

Chet   Good idea. And we can ask
          the people who live here
          if they know where
          the monster is hiding.

Adi   Er … you don't suppose there's any chance that the monster lives here, do you?

Chet   No way.

Adi   Okay, so why's the ground shaking, and what's that heavy thumping sound coming from behind the cottage?

Chet   I don't know. It's probably
an elephant bouncing
on a trampoline.

Adi   Right. So you don't think it's
a monster's footsteps then?

Chet   No!

Adi   And what do you think is making that huge shadow?

Chet   I don't know. It's probably somebody's pet gorilla.

Adi   Fine. So there's no way it could be the monster's huge shadow, then?

Chet   Of course it's not. It's …

Adi   What?

Chet   Run for your life – it's the monster!

Up, Up
and Awayeeee!

Adi and Chet jump back on their bikes
and begin to pedal like mad.
The monster chases after them.
They can hear its heavy footsteps
thumping close behind them.
But the monster can't catch them.
They're going too fast.

Chet   Keep on pedalling, Adi.
We're getting away.

Adi   Chet!

Chet   What is it, Adi?

Adi   There's a great big ditch
right in front of us.

Chet   Quick, let's turn back!

Adi   We can't – the monster's
right behind us. What are we
going to do?

Chet   There's only one thing for it.
            We'll have to do wheelies on our
            bikes and fly over the ditch.

Adi   But the ditch is really wide.

UP, UP AND AWAYEEEEE!

Chet   Good. *We'll* make it but
the monster won't. It'll never
be able to jump across.

Adi   Here we go.

Chet   Up, up and awayeeeee!

The boys speed through the air
on their bikes.

Chet	We're going to make it.
Adi	We're going to make it.
Chet	We're NOT going to make it.
Adi	Arghhhhhhh!

The bikes crash into the side of the ditch.
The boys whizz through the air.
They land on their feet on the far side
of the ditch.

They think they are safe, but the monster
runs at the ditch and takes a mighty leap.
It sails over the ditch and lands
with a bump on the other side.

Adi and Chet run away as fast as they can. The monster picks itself up and chases after them.

Monster Munch?

Adi and Chet can see Lee's uncle's house in the distance. They think if they can get there before the monster, they'll be safe. They run even faster.
Sweat is dripping down their faces, but they are nearly there.

Then Adi starts to run out of breath.
He slows down. Chet looks back
over his shoulder.

Chet   Don't give up now, Adi –
we're almost home.

Adi   Chet, watch out for that rock.

Chet   What rock are you talking about?
Arghhhh!

Adi   The rock you've just tripped over.
Arghhhh! Now *I've* tripped over
you!

The two boys lie in a heap
on the ground as the monster
dashes up to them. It skids to a halt
right next to them.

Adi   We're done for, Chet.
        The monster's caught us.

Chet   Yes! We nearly made it, but now
        we're going to be eaten alive.
        HELP!

But there is no one to help the boys.
They are doomed!

Adi and Chet look up at the monster.
It's as tall as a tree and covered in
green fur. It has claws and fangs
and eyes like bright red coals.
It opens its mouth, but
instead of roaring it says:

Monster I do love a game of tag.
And now, lads … it's your turn
to chase me!

About the author

Roger Hurn has:

 been an actor in 'The Exploding Trouser Company'

 played bass guitar in a rock band

been given the title Malam Oga (wise teacher, big boss!) while on a storytelling trip to Africa.

Now he's a writer, and he hopes you like reading about the Mystery Mob as much as he likes writing about them.

The monster quiz

Questions

1 Which monster has the nickname of 'Nessie'?

2 Which monster has trouble finding shoes to fit?

3 Why didn't the ghost go to the dance?

4 How do monsters tell their future?

5 What do you get if you cross a Vampire with the Abominable Snowman?

6 Why do witches use broomsticks to fly about on?

7 What's the best way of talking to a monster?

8 What do you give a vampire with a sore throat?

9 What do you call a monster wearing ear muffs?

10 What do you call glasses for a ghost?

Answers

1 The Loch Ness Monster.
2 Big Foot.
3 Because he had no body to go with.
4 They read their **horror**scopes.
5 Frostbite.
6 Because they'd look silly on vacuum cleaners.
7 By telephone.
8 Coffin drops.
9 Anything you like. It can't hear you.
10 Spooktacles.

How did you score?

- If you got all eight monster quiz answers correct, then you really are monster smart!

- If you got six monster quiz answers correct, then you can really tell your ghoulies from your ghosties (and long-leggedy beasties).

- If you got fewer than four monster quiz answers correct, then you've been monstered!

41

When I was a kid

Question Did you ever see a monster when you were a kid?

Roger Yes.

Question Did it scare you?

Roger No, in fact we became the best of **fiends**.

Question So what did you do together?

Roger We played the monster's favourite game.

Question What was that?

Roger Hide and Shriek.

Adi's favourite monster joke

Having an adventure

Must-dos and don'ts

Before you go on an adventure,
always tell your mum or dad
or whoever is looking after you.
Check with them if it's okay to go.

Don't go off on your own.
Adventures are more fun with friends.

Make sure you are wearing the right sort of
clothes and shoes or boots. (Otherwise you
might get blistered feet, soaking wet
or sunburn.)

Know how you're going to get there –
and how you're going to get home again.

Check the weather before you leave
and don't be afraid to come home from
your adventure if the weather turns bad.

Have emergency money – and that doesn't mean for sweets! It's for your bus fare home after the adventure.
(Even top adventurers get tired.)

 Always have your mobile phone with you in case you need to call for help (or for your mum to bring more sandwiches).

 Carry a whistle or an alarm with you at all times.

 Avoid talking to people you don't know or don't know well.

Monster lingo

Ghost The spirit of a dead person.
Ghosts who haunt tall buildings
are called high spirits.

Ghoul A ghost that haunts football pitches.
Ghouls are usually found in the net behind
the ghoul keeper.

Goblin A small magical creature
with bad table manners.

Spook A quiet ghost – it only spooks
when it's spooken to.

Vampire A well-dressed monster
who drinks blood. Most vampires are
just a pain in the neck.

Werewolf A normal person who
turns into a wolf at the full moon.
You can escape from a werewolf
by throwing a stick and yelling,
"Fetch it, boy!"

Witch A woman with magical powers,
a pointy hat, a cat and a broomstick.
When a lot of witches get together
it's hard to know which witch is which.

Zombie A big, shambling creature
that's totally brain dead –
just like Rob's big brother.

Mystery Mob